Ginny's Day

Lara Helmling

Illustrated by Katrina Koch

www.larahelmling/ginnys-day.com

ISBN: 0-9827992-3-3
ISBN-13: 978-0-9827992-3-9

Printed in the U.S.A.

DEDICATION

This book is dedicated to my grandparents,
Wallace and Reva Bean.
Grandma and Grandpa,
you have taught me how to live,
how to love, and how to grow old.

ACKNOWLEDGMENTS

I'd like to thank Shirley for the talks we've shared,
her love of dogs and her beautiful smile.

"Therefore we do not lose heart,
but though our outer man is decaying,
yet our inner man is being renewed day by day."

2 Corinthians 4:16 NASB

When Ginny woke up in the morning, she wasn't sure where she was. The white walls looked nothing like the soft blue of her bedroom. Was she in a hospital? Was she sick? Did she fall again? She hoped she hadn't hit her head.

She raised herself on her elbows and blinked several times. She couldn't imagine why she wouldn't know where she was. Some of the things in the room looked familiar. Come to think of it, they were hers. Her mother's small wooden desk was placed in front of a window. Pictures sat on top of the desk in brass frames. Christopher, Jennifer, and the grandchildren. Harold and her on the beach in Florida. Christopher on his first birthday. A small grainy black and white of Ginny and her older brother holding hands. All of these pictures were so familiar to her, but the room was not. She couldn't for the life of her think of why her furniture and pictures would be in a hospital room.

Ginny turned to her side and strained to sit up on the edge of the bed. She breathed hard with exertion. "God, please be with me," she prayed. "Help me not to fall again." As she caught her breath, she saw her slippers on the floor at the side of the bed. She teetered to her feet, catching the walker with her right hand. "I wonder who put that there," she said. Ginny put her slippers on and grabbed hold of the walker with both hands. Once she felt steady, she breathed a sigh of relief. "Thank you, Lord."

Suddenly, she remembered. Of course, this was her apartment. She lived in a senior home now. She shook her head. She said to herself, "How could I be so silly, to forget something like that?" Then she remembered that there was something special about today. Something special was supposed to happen. What was it? Ginny laughed to herself. "Well, I guess it's going to be a surprise," she said.

Ginny tottered out to the living room, pausing in the kitchenette to start the coffee pot. Her morning routine came back to her. She would get her coffee, sit down and watch some TV, and then she'd get her clothes on and comb her hair. Then she'd go out to breakfast. She hoped she could sit at her favorite table in the dining room. She liked to sit with Marge and Shirley at their table, but she just didn't care for the others. The others didn't seem to talk much, and Ginny just hated sitting there in a quiet room listening to old people chew.

It took Ginny an hour to get ready for breakfast, and then she really had to hurry. It was already 7:10. Everyone else would be sitting down and she wouldn't get her favorite place. She shuffled along behind her walker as fast as she could. She couldn't get over how long it took her to get ready in the morning. She used to be able to get ready in 15 minutes. She'd be in the car and on the road to the bank in no time flat. She was the manager of the whole bank when she retired.

Ginny's thoughts returned to the present. Ginny stopped and leaned on her walker. It seemed like something was going to happen today. There was a surprise. Or was that yesterday?

"Good morning, Ginny. Are you going to eat with us today?"

The voice startled Ginny out of her reverie. One of the nurses was smiling at her. Ginny smiled back. She looked around for a moment. "Do I have a surprise today?"

The nurse smiled and patted her hand. "I don't know. Is something special happening today?"

"I think so, but I just can't remember."

"You were just on your way to breakfast, weren't you?"

Ginny nodded. "Yes. Yes, I was."

"Well, your seat is all ready for you. And it's your favorite – you like to sit with Marge and Shirley, don't you?"

"Oh, yes, that's just where I want to be." Ginny spotted her friends and shuffled a little faster.

Another nurse came to take Ginny's order. "What would you like for breakfast this morning?"

"I'd just like oatmeal and bacon. Crisp, please."

"Crispy bacon and oatmeal. Okay, you got it. Don't you want any juice or milk?"

"Oh, orange juice. Yes, yes, I do. You remember, don't you?"

"I do, Miss Ginny. I remember you."

"Why, thank you. Aren't you nice." Ginny smiled encouragingly at her.

At breakfast, Ginny had told Marge and Shirley about the bank where she used to work. She enjoyed talking much more than eating. She ate, but food just didn't taste good anymore. She told them all about the duties she had and the ways that she had advised her clients. Marge and Shirley were very impressed. The nurses seemed more patronizing than anything, which irritated her. She had been a very important person, someone they would have seen as an authority. They would have treated her with deference and respect if they had come to her office back in that day. Not that she ever flaunted her power. She tried her best to help every customer who came in the door.

Marge and Shirley understood how important her job was. Ginny felt like a professional again as she talked about those days.

After breakfast, Ginny headed back to her apartment.

Ginny's favorite nurse approached her. "There's a choir coming to sing this morning in the living room. Are you going to come, Ginny?"

Ginny tried to think of the young nurse's name. She wished so much that she could remember. "No, honey, not today. I'm going to wait for my surprise. Something special is supposed to happen today."

"What's going to happen?"

"I can't remember, but I know it's something special."

"Why don't you come and then if your surprise comes, you can go back to your apartment."

"No, I'd better wait. Thank you."

The truth was, Ginny was already tired from breakfast. Now all she wanted was to rest.

She sat down heavily in her recliner. Oh, did that ever feel good. She thought about reading her Bible, like she had when she was younger. She had read the Bible through three times in her life. But somehow it didn't make sense anymore. She'd given up trying. She laid her head back and put her feet up. Before long, she was asleep.

Ginny dreamed about Harold. They were at their winter place in Florida, walking on the beach. That was their habit. Every morning of the world, they would walk barefoot, Ginny picking up seashells and Harold looking out to sea. There was a beeping sound there on the beach that seemed out of place. Suddenly, the dream changed and she was standing over Harold's hospital bed. The beeping heart monitor let her know he was still alive. Tears ran down her face. Then it was her son in the bed, her youngest son. Teddy. Why wouldn't he wake up? Wake up, Teddy. Wake up, honey.

She came awake suddenly. Oh Lord, to have Teddy in her arms again. What she wouldn't give for that moment. What she wouldn't give. She touched her wet cheek.

A nurse came into Ginny's apartment, startling her again.

"Did you knock?" asked Ginny.

"Of course, Ginny. Didn't you hear me knock?"

"No."

"I'm sorry, honey. It's time to take your medicine."

"I'd call to let you know it's all right to come in if you'd knock."

The nurse handed Ginny her medicine. "You like it when people knock, don't you?"

"Yes, I do." Ginny swallowed the handful of pills with the water. "Thank you, dear." She handed the glass back to the nurse. "Am I being cross today?"

"You're fine, darlin'.

"I don't want to be cross."

"You're all right. I heard your son is coming today."

"Teddy?"

"No, Christopher."

"Christopher!" Ginny paused to think about that. "Christopher is coming here? Today?"

"Yes, that's what he said. He said he'll be here at three."

"That's right. I knew that. That's what I've been waiting for today! It's been such a long time since I saw him."

"He was here just a few days ago."

"Oh, I think it's been longer than that. He's a good boy, you know. Very successful. Very busy. You know, kids these days, they're all so busy."

It was almost time for lunch, but Ginny wasn't hungry. All she could think of was that Christopher was coming to see her. She tried to remember how long it had been since he'd been here the last time. She just couldn't remember.

As she shuffled down to lunch behind her walker, she saw her friend from Sunday night movies and bingo.

"Hi, Marta. Christopher is coming today."

"Oh, well, that's exciting. Are you coming to play bingo with us at 4?"

"No, I won't be there today. Christopher said he'd be here at 3. I think it was three. Yes, three. So I won't be there."

"Have a wonderful visit, Ginny."

"Thank you, Marta, I will."

Ginny hurried back to her apartment after lunch just in case Christopher was early. It was almost 1:30 when she got in her chair. After ten minutes, he still hadn't come. Ginny thought maybe he would be there at 3 after all.

Why did Teddy have to die? She'd asked God that question so many times. The minister always said that God makes all things good. But what good could come of taking a child from his family? Ginny prayed, as she always did, that she would have peace in her heart. When she was younger, she would stay busy to keep the sadness at bay, but now there was nothing to stop the memories. Ginny cried and prayed until she fell asleep.

"Hi, Mom."

A man's voice lofted over Ginny, waking her from another dream.

"Mom."

Ginny opened her eyes. "Harold?"

"No, Mom. It's Christopher."

Ginny blinked at the man in front of her. He took her hand. "Christopher?"

"Hi, Mom."

"Oh, Christopher! I've been waiting for you."

Ginny glanced over at the clock. "Is it three o'clock already?"

"Yes, it is. Did you remember I was coming?"

"Oh, yes. The nurse reminded me, too."

"Good, I'm glad." Christopher pulled a kitchen chair over to sit beside her. "How are you, Momma?"

"Oh, fine, I guess. Don't you look handsome? In your nice slacks and tie."

"Yes, I had a business lunch today."

"How did it go?"

"Good. Very good. How are you feeling?"

"Oh, fine. I guess. Tired. I'm always tired, Christopher."

"I'm sorry."

"Do you think the doctors can do something about that?"

"I don't think so, Mom."

"Why am I so tired?"

"Well, you're just getting older."

"This old body is just giving out, isn't it?"

Christopher smiled and patted her hand.

Christopher was getting ready to leave. The time had gone so fast.

"When will you be back?" she'd asked.

"I'll be in here on Wednesdays and Saturdays, just like always. I promise you that, Mom."

"What day is it today?"

"Wednesday, Mom."

"Okay. So you'll be here Saturday."

"Yes, I will. Call me if you need anything before then, okay? Anything at all."

"I don't want to bother you. You're so busy with your beautiful family and your work."

"Don't worry about it. I want to be here for you. Anytime, okay? Promise?"

"Well, we'll see. I'm sure I'll be fine."

He'd kissed her and hugged her tightly. Ginny asked clung to him as he hugged her. "How long do you think life can go on this way, Christopher?"

Christopher held her tight. "I don't know, Mom. But I sure hope we have some more time. I'm not ready for you to go yet."

As Ginny pulled away, she thought she saw a tear glistening in the corner of his eye. "My sweet boy." She touched his cheek. "I love you, Christopher."

"I love you, too, Mom."

Christopher left at 4:30. He had to beat the traffic home, he said. Isabelle had a piano recital tonight. Oh, how she'd love to be healthy enough to go hear her. But she just couldn't do it anymore.

Now the apartment felt so empty without him. The silence and the emptiness seemed to overwhelm her. But he said he would be back on Saturday. She clung to that, and thought over all the things they'd talked about. She'd treasure those moments forever.

Somehow, another day had passed and Ginny was lying down to sleep. Her old body was just worn out. She thought back over the day, straining to remember every detail.

Christopher. Christopher had come today. She was so glad to have had such a nice visit with him. He would always be her boy, no matter how successful or strong he was now. She thanked God for Christopher.

Smiling happily and humming to herself, she fell asleep.

BOOK CLUB QUESTIONS

1. Many family caregivers experience a lot of guilt for not doing more for their elderly parents. However, research indicates that family caregivers like Christopher shouldn't feel guilty. Why shouldn't Christopher feel guilty about limiting his visits with his elderly mother to twice a week.

2. Ginny lives in a very well-managed and person-centered eldercare facility. What do you notice about the facility that is person-centered? What signs indicate that it is well-managed?

3. What should family caregivers look for in a facility when they are choosing one for their elderly parent?

4. Many elderly parents in Ginny's age group want to remain living in their homes alone. What in Ginny's health and mental capacity indicates that she is no longer capable of safely and healthily living alone?

5. In reality, all interactions with elderly parents aren't ideal. Elderly parents are often difficult because of their memory issues and their frustrations over their limitations. What are some good techniques to help caregivers be patient with both their parents and themselves when conflicts occur?

6. Why do you think that Christopher chose to have his mom live in a care facility instead of at his home? What are the advantages and disadvantages of having an elderly parent in a care facility instead of at home with family caregivers?

7. What other questions do you imagine that Christopher might have asked his mother during their visit?

For discussions on these questions and more caregiving tips, please visit:
larahelmling.com/free-caregiving-info.

ABOUT THE AUTHOR

Lara Helmling is a Christian and a wife, mother and author.
She also leads The Jesus Files ministry.
She has a special place in her heart
for the precious souls that are the most vulnerable,
such as the elderly and children.

ABOUT THE ARTIST

Katrina Koch is an artist who is pursuing
her college degree in art. She began drawing at age 14
when her mother told her one of her drawings was ugly.
Katrina drew the character over and over to prove her wrong.
She has since drawn hundreds of faces,
all of which she knows are beautiful.